To Santiago

A Dog's Tale

A Furry Farm Fantasy

By Susan Curry

Ideas and Illustrations by Isla B

I hope you enjoy this story,

Susan

Across Ocean Books, Davis, CA
www.acrossoceanbooks.com

ISBN: 978-0-944176-06-1
Printed in the United States of America

CATALOGING INFORMATION:
Curry, Susan
A Dog's Tale: A Furry Farm Fantasy

FILING CATEGORIES:

JUV002070 JUVENILE FICTION/Animals/Dogs
JUV002090 JUVENILE FICTION/
   Animals/Farm Animals
PET004010 PETS/Dogs/Breeds
PET004020 PETS/Dogs/Training

To animal lovers everywhere

Table of Contents

Chapter 1 – A Mishap

I was down at the barn talking with the ducks when I smelled melting butter. Of course, silly me, it was Saturday, pancake day. Barking goodbye to my feathered friends, I bounded across the yard and to the kitchen, my favorite room in the farmhouse. Lizzie, our mom, is the best cook I know, though I don't get to taste it much because my entire diet is dog food. Good quality but rather boring, day after day. I have to rely on baby Summer to drop tasty bits onto the floor. Mom calls me her furry vacuum cleaner.

I must have lost concentration for a moment, because as I reached the doorway my paws slipped and I skidded right across the room to mom. My bottom hurt, and I'd banged one of my paws on the table leg, but I squashed my yelp because I didn't want Lizzie to stop cooking to check me over. I would survive this.

As I looked around, I noticed that the whole family was at the table. Not only that, they were trying hard not to smile at my sudden entry. How embarrassing. But Emma, the kind twelve-year-old who loves animals more than anyone I know, rushed around the table to see if I was all right.

She poked and prodded, then said, "You're OK, Sheila. No broken bones. Just as well, because we're going to the county fair today. You won't be happy that I'll have to give you a bath and a haircut, but after that we'll practice our walk in front of the judges."

She was right: I wasn't happy about the bath one little bit, but I did enjoy showing off my skills to an audience, and had won Best-in-Show twice in the past. While I was thinking about her announcement, mom turned suddenly with a spatula in her hand, and on that spatula was a pancake, golden brown and giving off a delicious smell.

Chapter 2 – RIVALRY

It smelled so good that I found myself drooling.

"Pancake number one! This goes to the person who can sit up the straightest. Emma, you don't need to compete. I'm so sorry that I don't have any gluten-free flour this morning. I have a boiled egg for you."

Emma scowled and whispered for the umpteenth time since her diagnosis, "I hate Celiac disease."

Dad smiled at mom and sat up straight.

"Thank you Derek," she said, and sent him an air kiss. Michael rolled his eyes.

"This is childish," he said.

The kiss, or the sitting up straight part? I wasn't sure.

"Of course it's childish. But it's a bit of fun for the little ones. You used to love a challenge like that when you were their age," said Lizzie.

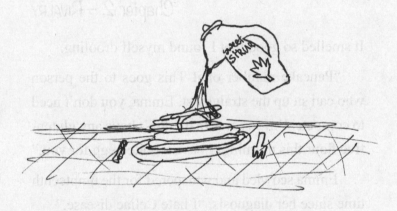

Saturday was pancake day

"Baby Summer is sitting up nicely. I'll give her the pancake. Michael, you can have the last one."

Michael's face went red.

"No fair," he said. "I'm the oldest."

Four-year-old Charlie, who thought Michael was cool and tried to imitate him whenever he could, said, "No fair. I'm older than Summer."

Dad looked at both of them with an expression of humor mixed with annoyance. The fifteen-year-old who was already shaving most mornings and was taller than both of his parents seemed suddenly younger. And Charlie, who, with his blond hair, brown eyes and rather unsuccessful swagger, was the spitting image of the younger Michael shown in photos.

Dad spoke kindly but firmly, "You're both right. You're both older than Summer and that's why mom and I rely on you to set a good example for her. I suggest you think this over while you are waiting."

Michael kept his eyes on his plate, looking as though he'd rather be anywhere but there. Charlie did the same, so quick about it that his forehead hit the plate. Everybody laughed, even Michael. The anger disappeared.

I was happy that Summer was quiet this morning, apart from practising her new words. She did this everywhere we went. Today it was "pa-cayk." She was often loud, and cried when she didn't like what was put in front of her, or wanted to get out of her high chair before we'd finished. But that day she seemed contented, and dropped several pieces of pancake down to me. Some were half-eaten, but I didn't mind. I felt some stickiness on my coat, but that didn't matter either. Emma would bathe me soon.

Chapter 3 – FIFTEEN

You may have noticed that sometimes I call the parents by their adult names: Derek and Lizzie; at other times I call them mom and dad. I'm not sure why I do this: maybe it's because I often see them just as adults, but at other times, when I'm feeling lonely, I like to think they are my actual parents. Sometimes I get it mixed up, but don't worry. It doesn't matter because they don't know what I'm thinking anyway.

So....back to my thoughts at the pancake breakfast. I felt sorry for dad, and also mom, who had enough to do keeping the farm going, food on the table, and all the other necessities of life, without worrying about how Michael was turning out. Fifteen can be a difficult age. Rosie, my shepherd dog friend who used to live next door, once told me about the difficulties they'd had with their daughter. It happened a few years before I was born. Jessica

Wilson, who'd been a child anyone would be proud of until she turned fifteen, changed almost overnight after falling in love with one of the men who delivered hay and other supplies.

Rosie said, "Your mom didn't believe it could be real. I remember thinking that she sounded a bit mean, which was unusual for her."

Lizzie had said, "She's only fifteen. It's nothing more than puppy love, a crush. It won't last long."

What's puppy love, I thought. It sounded insulting. But Rosie kept talking, so I let it go.

"Of course the romance didn't last," she said. "The delivery man looked about thirty – really old – and already had a wife and family. The romance was one-sided from the start. In the end, Jessica gave in to her parents, finished school, went off to college and married someone her own age. They live just a few miles away."

"Then why haven't I seen her visiting?" I asked.

"I can't be sure, but I think that the troubles earlier in her teenage years left her with a grudge which hasn't changed."

After she told me this story she said, "You may wonder how I knew about this episode. I can't

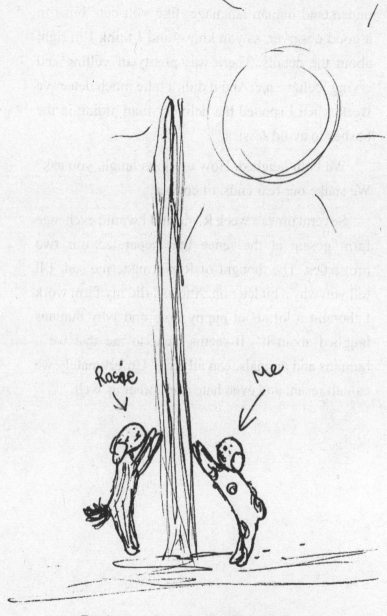

Rosie and Sheila talked by the fence

understand human language, like you can, but I'm a good observer, as you know, and I think I'm right about the details. There was plenty of yelling and crying, believe me. And it didn't take much detective work when I spotted the delivery man hiding in the bushes to avoid Jessica."

We both laughed. How do dogs laugh, you ask? We shake our rear ends, of course.

Several times a week Rosie and I would exchange farm gossip at the fence that separated our two properties. The thought of Rosie made me sad. I'll tell you why a bit later on. And as I did my farm work I thought a lot about puppy love and why humans laughed about it. It seems clear to me that we – humans and animals, can all love. Unfortunately we can all resent and even hate each other as well.

It seemed to me that mom had made more pancakes than usual, or that Summer had dropped more pieces than usual. My tummy was full, so it took a little longer for me to walk to the gate to fetch the newspaper. It didn't matter: spring flowers were everywhere and there was a soft, cool breeze to make it a pleasant walk. I tried not to drool on the paper, but after a while the wind dropped, and when I thought of cool water, saliva rushed into my mouth. Emma was waiting for me on the step with a bottle of shampoo, another of conditioner, a brush and comb set, scissors and a couple of towels.

She turned away from me, quickly wiped off the saliva with the back of her hand, and glanced at the newspaper headlines.

"There are several articles about the main event of the weekend. We're very lucky. The weather report says it will be sunny all day. I'm glad you won't have to chase sheep in the rain."

Actually, I never mind the rain, but it would be complicated to try to tell her that, so I just put on my best smile.

"My dear doggy," she said, "sometimes I think you understand everything I say."

She hugged me tight. She's right of course. I do understand everything she says, and have done so for some time. And not only Emma. I can understand any human if they speak clearly. When I get frustrated, my best move is to stare at her with my one blue eye and my one brown eye. Her giggle makes me happy every time I do it.

Some people don't know that many Australian Shepherds have eyes that are differently colored from each other. I'm very proud of my eye color, or should I say colors, and my red Merle (multi-colored) coat which feels so soft when I'm cleaned up. And how do I know about these features? It's not as if there's a mirror in the barn. Whenever we meet someone new, Emma can't resist boasting about the colors of my eyes and coat.

When I was born on this ranch about five years ago, it turned out to be good timing for Emma. She had been lonely, after Michael started fifth grade and had more homework than ever. Dad, mom and several other parents complained to the teacher, but nothing changed, so Michael wasn't as free after school to play with her as they used to do. However, I heard our parents talking one night after I was supposed to be asleep on my brown, soft doggie bed. It seemed they'd talked to Michael's teacher, Mr. Rolland, and now believed that Michael had been exaggerating. In Mr. Rolland's opinion, Michael had gone through a growth spurt recently, and had probably lost interest in playing Emma's games. Mom and dad began to watch how Michael filled in his after-school time before chores and dinner. Sure enough, he stretched out his homework time by taking several breaks for snacks and drinks, and playing online computer games with his friends.

Chapter 5 – My Big Leap Forward

After a time of frustration and hurt at Michael's change, Emma turned to me even more. She played imaginary games with me, and pretended that I could understand everything she said. Mom and dad noticed that Emma was developing into a real animal lover, and encouraged her to be responsible for my training. This was a great success. Dad said that his goal for me was that I'd become the best working dog ever. That meant that Emma and I had to cut back the times we played, because I now had an important role. I heard dad telling his brother on the phone that because I am a purebred, if I didn't get trained as a herding dog, I would be a problem, because Aussies love to work, love to run, and are quick learners. If they don't have anything to do they can cause mischief.

One Aussie they had was a disappointment. He'd nipped the sheep, sometimes deeply, which of course ruined the wool. Dad looked into it and found that the previous owners didn't bother training him. They just expected that he would know what to do. Dad was furious, and had to find a home for him in town. At the time I was just coming out of puppy-hood, so dad pounced on me to be the Merchant family's wonder dog.

Emma and I spent her hours after school of training time together until I knew what all of her signals meant, and was able to respond quickly. Soon I was able to hustle those dumb sheep into the barn for shearing, or to another part of our land with tasty new grass for them to eat.

Rosie was amazed that I'd picked up people talk. It happened so quickly and I don't know how. One morning I just could. Possibly it was because Emma often read to me. These were short books with lots of pictures. It wasn't hard to piece the pictures and the story together with her voice. I'm rather unusual, perhaps unique. I've never met a dog whose owner reads to them. My only wish now is that I could talk back, but that's not likely to happen any time soon. I'd love to see Emma's face if my silly tongue didn't get in the way of speech, and I could have real conversations with her. But if I had a tantrum over it nobody would know what I was trying to say. Something like aarrrrgghh.

Emma scrubbed Sheila all over

Chapter 6 – The Bath

Emma put Summer's wading pool on the lawn and filled it partway with cold water. She put a finger in and said, "It's too cold. I'll get some hot water from the kitchen." I was grateful. It was still sunny but the breeze had picked up again. First, Emma took special care to remove the little sticks and burrs on my coat, by pulling the comb slowly through my mass of fur. It's so thick that if she pulled too hard, it would hurt. Then she helped me into the wading pool to scrub and rinse me. She was excited and couldn't stop talking.

"You're going to look terrific today, Sheila! I'm certain that you'll not only be Best-in-Show, but you could win the sheepdog trial as well." What she didn't know is that my paw was still hurting from the bump at breakfast. I worried that I would disappoint her. She saw my worried face and distracted me by the game we always played when the bath was over.

She'd try to rub me all over with a towel, while I played getaway. She always won, but I didn't care. It was fun!

Mom came out with Charlie in her arms. She plopped him down and leaned over to feel my fur.

"Emma," she said, I'll get the extension cord and the hair dryer. It's a bit too cool to have Sheila dry naturally." I hated the dryer's loud noise. It was all I could do not to whine like a puppy. But it was soon done, and Emma gave me a tasty doggie treat. The treat made the ordeal almost worth it.

At last I was dry, combed and trimmed. I felt like a fluffy puppy again.

"Now don't go rolling in the dirt," Emma warned. I was a bit offended until I remembered doing it the last time she groomed me. She has a very good memory.

"You have to stay pretty, just until after the dog trials. I stared at her watch, and she noticed. "It's nearly 11 o'clock, so you'll have to stay clean until we leave at 1:30." I didn't know how long that would be, but I suspected it would be a while, so I lay down on the patch of grass near the front door and fell asleep in the sun.

Chapter 7 – News

I was dreaming that mom was putting tuna and dog food in my bowl when I heard voices. The dream was so real that I almost ran inside to see if she had. In reality she was holding the newspaper and frowning.

"Here's some unexpected news, Emma. Do you remember that the Wilsons next door have ordered an Aussie to replace Rosie? Well, they thought it would take a few months, but someone canceled their order at the breeder and the Wilsons picked up the dog yesterday at the airport. It seems that it came all the way from Arizona. Edith Wilson told me just a few minutes ago, and it's here in the paper too. Apparently he's a champion." Emma was quiet for a moment, then said slowly,

"Well, I suppose we'll get used to him as time goes on. He might be a friend to Sheila and help her get over missing Rosie so much." But she didn't look as though she believed it. I was confused. Why did mom look unhappy? Why did Emma say something she didn't believe? I was glad when Emma asked mom what was wrong.

"Because they are entering him in the events this afternoon. Seems to me that it's too soon, but I'm worried that he and Sheila will have to do the two-dog trial without having practiced beforehand."

Emma looked shocked, and replied,

"Then the Wilsons shouldn't have him in that event. Can you ask them to withdraw him? We could ask Eliza Bennett if Buster could substitute. At least he and Sheila know each other."

Mom looked doubtful. "I don't know if it's possible. You know how competitive the Wilsons are. They won't want to withdraw a champion, now that he's arrived just in time. I'll have a talk to dad and we can decide once we've had a look at Rufus – that's his name."

She was soon back.

"Dad has just talked to Joe Wilson, and I also saw Rufus from a distance. He looks younger and is already bigger than Sheila. He was returned to the breeder by a family that found him too active.

What did they expect? He was constantly wanting a walk. Their little children went flying when he ran from one end of the house to the other. And it was a small house. Joe is excited because Rufus has won competitions all over the state. The downside is that they'll have to work on his attitude. He comes with a reputation of needing to be the alpha dog – with any dog. And he can be aggressive sometimes."

Dad came to her, and said, "Joe agreed that Sheila and Rufus should not work together in the two-dog event, so we are taking them both out. The Bennetts are on vacation."

His words made me sadder than ever that Rosie wouldn't be with me. It wasn't fair that I had to withdraw just because of Rufus. The Wilsons shouldn't have sold Rosie away to a family in town, just because she was not as fast as she used to be. We had worked as a team since Emma started training me.

I'll never forget the day that Rosie left. She was looking straight at me from the back window of the Wilsons' car, and as she opened and shut her mouth I imagined she was pleading, "Save me!"

Thinking of Rosie made me restless and unable to go back to sleep. I hoped 1:30 would come around quickly. Remembering what mom and dad told us often, I looked for an upside to change. A new dog in the district could be fun, but we knew nothing about Rufus as yet, except that he liked to be the alpha dog. I didn't like the sound of it: that was MY position. I hoped he wouldn't be TOO TOO outstanding.

Chapter 8 – WHAT A DAY!

I'd like to let you know what happened at the fair, where all of our hopes were turned upside down. I'm still upset by it, but it might help if I sift through the events which were part of it.

Dad, Emma, Michael and I left early, so I don't know what mom, Charlie and Summer did after we left, so I'm going to guess. I love to tell stories: my barn friends will agree. This is what I think might have happened until we met at the fair.

I imagine that little Charlie woke from his nap that afternoon to find the house unusually quiet. Although he knew that his family was to go to town that afternoon for the fair, he panicked as he looked out the window and saw mom waving goodbye to us as the truck headed downhill to the gate. This was a terrible blow. Since Summer was born eighteen months before, Charlie had come to think of himself as one of the big kids. His legs were still short, but most of the time he managed to keep up with the older children. He could ride a horse if someone was with him, and was able to spring from hay bale to hay bale in the barn with Emma, playing his favorite game, "come and get me."

On weekends when there was no preschool he spent most of his time either trailing behind mom, or playing outside with me. And if Michael was in a good mood, he taught Charlie computer games.

Now Charlie was really upset. He ran outside with tears falling fast, and shouted angrily at mom,

"How could they go without me? I want to see the sheepdog trials." I imagine that mom would soothe him. She's good at that. She most likely squatted down, wrapped her arms around him, and whispered in his ear.

"Don't cry, they had to get there early. As soon as Summer wakes up, we'll drive to join them. But since your feelings are hurt, how would you like a bowl of strawberry ice cream before we leave?" She always has some treats ready for anyone who needs a boost, and her hugs are warm and caring.

Charlie would have stopped crying right away.

"Are you sure we won't miss out seeing the doggies?" he asked.

"I'm really, really sure," said mom, and took his hand as they walked back to the house.

Just then they heard a waking-up sort of cry from Summer, who looked around and said loudly, "Seila? Where Seila?" They all dressed quickly and gobbled down the ice cream before piling into the Forester.

It was a fifteen-minute trip to town, and usually a quiet ride. But today there was dense traffic, and even a mile or two out they could hear music and crowd noise. Charlie's excitement was growing. He had been talking to Emma about the fair for weeks now, and asked mom the important questions.

"Will they have sausages on sticks? Will they have apple tarts? They're my favorites!"

"They always do," answered mom. She may have been surprised that Charlie still remembered the menu from a whole year before, and I too have noticed that he has a good memory for a four-year-old.

From her car seat, Summer was trying out some new words: "i-ceem, sausgez, appw tars." Charlie laughed with delight, and said, "Summer, you'll soon be as smart as me."

Now it was Lizzie's turn to laugh.

They drove up to the gate which led to the car park. Gerry Paulson, who always directed drivers to parking places at big events, looked into the car and said to mom, "The rest of your family is over there. The dogs are getting ready for judging. I've put my money on Sheila to take all the prizes today."

"We all hope so," Lizzie said, "especially for Emma's sake. She puts so much work into getting Sheila ready for this." (That's the end of my made-up story. I hope you liked it. I love making up stories. The rest of what I'm telling you really happened).

They soon found Derek and Michael leaning against the fence that had been put up for the contest. The fence formed a circle, and on the outer side opposite, a flock of about twenty sheep bleated nervously within a small enclosure. Lizzie looked closely at Derek and Michael's faces, which appeared unhappy, then took in the entire scene. I watched her and was not surprised at all to find that she was looking at me, then at a dog we hadn't seen before, most likely Rufus, then back again to me, as though she were guessing which might win Best-in-Show. I imagined that she had eliminated the rest of the dogs, and agreed with her. They were a bunch of losers.

Most of the dogs were a bunch of losers

Some had fur over their faces, so they could hardly see. I know that for some breeds that's normal, but someone should have added a pony tail holder so the poor animal would stop running into things. I noticed that mom and dad looked worried when old Fred Perkins walked by with his very smelly dog. As he passed, we all realized that Fred was smelly too. I heard Derek say quietly, "He's losing it. It's so sad. Since his wife died he's gone downhill."

One dog had a limp, another strained on her leash impatiently. As far as I could tell, Rufus and I were the best of the bunch. The big question was: could he be as well-behaved as I was?

Emma was in the parade, holding my leash. Every dog, even the best behaved like me, had to be on a leash. When dogs are anxious, you never know what they will do. Whenever Emma looked at Rufus she looked scared. I raised my head to look at her, and smiled to give her support. She tried to smile back, but she looked pale. After looking at the other dogs again, she seemed to be gathering courage, and said with a determined look, "we can do it."

Chapter 9 – THE JUDGES

I wonder if you are asking why Shepherds are in a Best-in-Show lineup. Good question. Sheepdog competitions are always judged by herding skills, but in a small town like this, anything goes. Anyway, dog breeds are not judged against each other. Instead they are judged against their own breed. Because Rufus and I were the only sheepdogs, we would be judged against each other.

We paraded round and round, slowly, standing at equal distances apart. The judges came to us one by one. The first, a tall woman who I'd seen with her Springer Spaniels many times, began checking my body. She gave me a quick rub all over and moved on. Emma took a deep breath: that was a good sign. We walked slowly to the next judge, an old man with a limp. He had a frown on his face, and I wondered if he had a stomach ache, or if he was unhappy with having only two well-groomed dogs to judge. After feeling each leg he told Emma to lead me around the ring so he could see how I walked. This is called gait. Despite my goal of walking easily, I have to admit that it was more difficult than I'd expected, due to my small accident that morning. I worried that he might mark me down.

While this was happening, I noticed that the third judge was watching the whole group, looking for attitude. Emma had told me all of this as part of my training.

Rufus and I looked spiffy. Our Merle coats of different colors – his was blue merle, while mine was red – were shining and trimmed, and free of insects and burrs. But I could tell that Rufus didn't understand human language, because while Mr. Wilson was telling the judge about me, the local champion, Rufus was distracted. He was an impatient dog. I'd noticed ponies like that, bored with giving rides to small children and itching to escape. When working closely with humans as I do, you need to pay attention to every word.

I was pretty sure that Rufus didn't have his heart in it. He may have been very tired after his flight, and I imagined that traveling in the cargo area of the plane would scare him badly. I began to feel a little sorry for him, but as we left the ring he snarled at me. I quickly changed my mind and sent bad thoughts instead. The judges told everyone that they would announce the winner after the sheepdog trials. Emma bent down to give me a hug and whispered, "Good luck, work hard on those sheep, and watch me for our signals."

Rufus distracted Sheila

Chapter 10 – SHAME

Later, on the way home, dad, Michael and Emma rehashed the events of the afternoon. I took myself to the back seat, turned my face to the window and tried not to hear them. I'd been doing well rounding up the sheep until Rufus distracted me by barking at his small flock and herding them in the direction of the river. Something Rufus didn't know was that the river wasn't safe, especially after the recent winter rains. Even in summer, it was dangerous for small children and animals to try even to walk across, let alone swim. Everyone knows that sheep are not very bright, so it was likely that they would go wherever Rufus took them.

Fortunately, the sheep's owner ran and stopped Rufus just as Mr. Wilson did the same. The two men exchanged angry words, then Mr. Wilson put a leash on Rufus and came back to the viewing area. By that time, my concentration was lost and my little flock had flown in all directions. I was so ashamed that I would have cheerfully walked home rather than hear my family's disappointment at my performance. I expected that Rufus would win the title of Best-in-Show as well. My leg injury was a defect, and Rufus' body was perfect.

But the judges had to take into account his bad behavior. For the first time ever, the main judge announced that no dog came up to requirements. The judges weren't giving out the Award at all. There was a big sigh of disappointment from the crowd, like air rushing out of a balloon. Then, as there were no more events to watch, most drifted away in their cars, or played games in the arcade, such as Whac-A-Mole, or rode the Carousel. The highlight of the afternoon for Charlie was that he won a huge brown bear, which he hugged closely as he ate his apple tart.

He was the only happy one, though. We left soon after that. I felt like a failure and tried to keep my ears closed, but from time to time I heard snatches of conversation: "…not up to her usual performance," (Michael). "I agree, but she might have been so scared about what Rufus was doing that she lost her concentration."(Derek). Then from Emma, "How can you say those things about her? She had a damaged paw, which wasn't her fault, and Rufus distracted her right when she was about to get every last sheep into the barn. I'd rather have a dog that cared about other creatures, not one who shows off and could have killed them." Michael looked at dad as if to say more, but I heard dad whisper, "Enough." Hmmmm. That was kind. I wondered if he knew I could understand what they were saying.

We drove slowly up the hill to our house, and dad pulled up at the barn. He patted me and asked,

"Sheila, would you like to eat with your farm friends tonight? You look pretty tired."

I crawled out of the back seat and slunk over to the ducks, feeling the worst I'd ever felt. I was a failure. Dad would probably do what the Wilsons did, and send me to another young child who wanted an older Australian Shepherd. I might have looked older, but I was not old at all, just exhausted.

As my imagination ran wild, I thought that dad and the Wilsons might save money by sharing one dog, and I would be the one to go. Then Rufus would become alpha dog without even trying.

Just as dad was climbing into the truck, he said aloud, as if to himself,

"Well, Sheila, you didn't win the contest, but take note, neither did Rufus. I thought he was very poorly behaved for a dog who is supposed to be a champion. Joe Wilson is quite upset." His words shocked me. I had been blaming myself for all that had happened.

I was grateful that none of my barn friends said anything, though they gathered around me with questioning looks. I must have looked a mess, with my fur all ruffled up and my sad look.

"I'll tell you all about it in the morning," I said. "I'm exhausted." They backed off, chattering among themselves. Dad brought my dinner, which I ate in a hurry, and then dragged myself wearily to one of the horse stalls and pushed some straw into a pile to make a bed. The barn was very quiet. Even the baby ducks stopped fighting and we all quickly fell asleep.

Chapter 11 – Gossip

I woke suddenly when the old red rooster, Cyril, crowed loudly. Of course he did that every day, but I hadn't been so close to him when he did. There was no going back to sleep now. I looked outside and saw that it was barely light, then heard Cyril scratching around next to me. He wanted to wake me up, that was for sure. I knew him to be a terrible gossip, and at first was angry that he was obviously wanting the story from yesterday. Then I realized that it might be an advantage to have Cyril spread the news. That would save me from having to tell it more than once. Unfortunately, I learned later that Cyril didn't have a very good memory. The details when he talked to Beatrice, the old cow, were changed.

She came up to me later in the morning and said, "I'm sorry to hear that Rufus deliberately scratched your leg. Next time I see him, I'll kick him." I don't think she was listening when I told her it wasn't true. At least Oswald, the very smart owl who lived in the barn rafters, had heard me talking to Cyril, and remembered the story as I did. He might also understand human language, I thought. I decided to discuss it with him when this was all over.

Though I was a little hurt by being gossiped about, I was glad that I wouldn't have to explain to my barn friends more than once why I was so sad. Even the black horse, Moonlight, who was usually unfriendly to me, tossed his head angrily as my friends discussed the way Rufus sabotaged my success when he took off towards the river.

"Next time I see Rufus I'll run towards him so fast that it'll scare him to death. If he gets hurt I won't shed one tear," he said loudly. I thought that was a bit strong, but there was a little part of me which agreed, and if Moonlight did take revenge, I decided I would do nothing to stop him.

For the next couple of days, I kept a low profile, as Emma would say. I don't know what a profile is, but she seems to understand when I want to be alone. I still felt like a failure, even though she was as nice to me as ever.

Sheila's barn friends gossiped about
what happened

Dad also was sensitive to my mood and gave me some time off. This gave me the chance to think through what had happened, and get some rest. By the end of the week, after consulting with wise Oswald, I decided to confront Rufus and give him a piece of my mind. It wasn't time to get Beatrice and Moonlight involved yet, though they'd be my backups if Rufus didn't listen.

Chapter 12 – EMERGENCY

I need to tell you about a very strange thing that happened to me while I was getting my strength back. It started when mom went to pick up Summer from her afternoon nap. When Summer hadn't cried on waking up, as she always did, mom finished answering emails and noticed that the hands on the old clock on the mantle had moved well past wake up time. As she stood in the doorway of Summer's room, she was shocked to find that her daughter was gone. I happened to be lying in the living room at the time, half asleep, but woke up quickly and rushed to mom, who was frantic.

I realized that what she needed was dad, not me, so I ran outside to find him. After a hasty search, I asked the barn animals if they knew where he'd gone.

According to Oswald, who'd heard mom and dad talking, he'd gone into town to buy a new water pump and groceries, and wouldn't be back until dinner time. It was then that I remembered that dad went to town every week.

Michael and Emma weren't home from school yet. Their bus always arrived two hours before dinner. I herded Charlie, who'd followed me outside, into the house and found mom. She took one look at my helpful face and realized in an instant that I was offering to look for Summer. She gave me a grateful look, picked up Charlie and followed me outside.

"OK Sheila. Lead the way," she said. The day had become gloomy, with huge clouds rushing by. It was still hot and humid, but the sky was darkening and I suspected it would rain soon. I could tell that mom was worried about this as well. What if the night turned cold and rainy? How would Summer survive in her flimsy pajamas? If there was lightning she would be terrified.

Mom pulled out her cell phone and talked to dad as we walked along, keeping our eyes peeled.

"I knew she was almost big enough to climb out of her crib," she told him, "but was hoping we might have had a few more months before she did it. It's my fault!" She burst into tears. I could hear dad's less panicked reply. "Don't worry, she can't have gone far on those little legs. I'm walking to the truck right now, and should be home in half an hour. Which direction are you walking?"

"We're heading towards the river. You know, where we often walk. But what if she went down the hill towards the road? She loved the fair so much that she might try to go back there."

As she said this, she cried even louder. Charlie cried too as he realized that this was a big deal.

Dad said, "I'll pick up Michael and Emma and let you know when we're home. There's cell phone reception for a mile or so around our place. Just keep walking." I realized a few minutes later that we'd gone quite a distance, and Summer wouldn't be this far away. It's hilly around here and she would have to scramble on her little legs. It had only been a few months since she could walk at all.

Just then, a puff of wind brought a new, wild scent to my nose. I ran through the animal smells that I knew: fox, coyote, horse, but not one of them fit. I stopped and waited for another breath of wind, and this time I knew what it was. Deer. There are many deer on the ranch but we don't see them very often.

Dad lets people hunt them sometimes when there are too many or he needs extra money, but Emma hates that, and she is always pestering dad to stop letting these beautiful, gentle creatures be shot.

The scent was moving a little to the right, and I followed it.

"Come back here," called mom. "We need to stay on the trail." I ignored her. Perhaps a deer might have seen Summer. They're very observant, always looking for danger. Mom kept yelling at me to come back. She was getting on my "last nerve," as Michael would say, but I had to find that deer. Now I thought I heard crying, and just then I saw something that blew my mind. Mom had been running after me and saw it at the same time. She screamed. Summer was sitting and crying under a tall bush, with a young, but large, deer, complete with antlers, standing close by. My first thought was that Summer was in danger. Mom certainly believed it. But I had to check, so I walked slowly up to the buck.

Chapter 13 – WHAT END IS UP?

With a shock, I realized that it was Harold, the son of my friend Gracie. Last time I'd seen him was when he was very young and of course had no antlers at the time. When I asked him to explain what was happening, he told me he'd found Summer wandering along the path quite a way back, and he'd stood by to wait and see if someone would come to rescue her. He looked agitated, and I asked him if anything was wrong. "As wrong as it can possibly be. My mother was shot and killed a few days ago, a hunting day on your property." I saw tears falling down and he shook his head to get rid of the tears. I moved back a little from his antlers.

"When I saw the child I guessed right away that she was from your Coastal E Ranch. What good timing, I thought." "What do you mean?" I asked. A

Sheila had met Harold, the deer, before

mean expression came over his face. I already knew what he had in mind, but I let him say the words.

"I realized that I could take revenge against your cruel owner who let a hunter kill my mother."

"How did you plan to do that?" I asked. Now I was getting worried. He seemed to be serious."

"I picked her up and brought her to this area where no one comes. I planned to just let her die." I told him that I was sorry, but I needed to say more than that, so I took a risk and told him I would do my best to stop the hunting. I had no plan for this, but hoped that something would come to me when I was with Emma. Harold relaxed, but he still looked determined.

"I'll hold you to it, Sheila. And the child can live, for now." He walked away. Mom was waiting on the path, terrified. I ran back to Summer, then back to mom a few times, until she realized that I wanted her to come and pick up her little daughter.

We were almost home again before dad, Michael and Emma found us. Mom was still recovering from the encounter with Harold, but she cheered up when telling the fantastic rescue story. Emma said,

"I'm upset that we missed all the excitement. But dad, don't let any more hunters onto our property!

I think that deer was protecting Summer." I looked up into Emma's eyes, and saw anxiety mixed with purpose. I was fairly sure she would work on dad to get the job done.

"I'll think about it," said dad. "There's a lot to consider." From the thoughtful expression on his face, though, I was hopeful.

At home Emma and Michael thawed out frozen pizzas in the microwave. Everyone was ravenous. Mom gave me a special meal of dog food with tuna mixed in it, my favorite, and made a short speech about my bravery in confronting the deer. She would never know that I'd met Harold before, or that he'd been thinking of hurting Summer. Instead I basked in the praise that came my way. Summer didn't seem to understand why we had all been panicked, and said over and over again, "Where dee?" Derek made her some antlers with construction paper, which Summer showed off until bedtime. The next day, the mattress in her crib had been lowered, and a sign on her door read, "Please close the door after you."

****

I've had detailed dreams before, but this one seemed so real that it was hard at first to separate what was real and what wasn't. I woke up slowly, but ready to run to help mom find Summer, then heard the toddler singing in her crib. It was such a long dream, and so strong that I lay on my bed for quite a while before I could get my head clear.

It was tempting to believe that Summer's disappearance actually happened, because the part where Harold the deer came into it was so interesting. But when I thought it over, I knew that nothing like that could happen. No deer would come as close to a child as Harold had, let alone threaten anyone. I shook myself a few times and went to find mum. On the way I passed Summer's room. There was no sign taped on the door. There were no pizza boxes in the recycle bin, either. I was disappointed to know that I didn't get any praise for a rescue, because there wasn't one. On the other hand, it wasn't my responsibility to convince dad to stop the hunting. I'd leave that to Emma.

Chapter 14 – Shearing Time

After the drama of the dog trials, we went back to our usual activities. It was shearing time for dad, and this meant sheep roundup time for me. I was very happy. Herding dogs like us love to be busy and love to help. I was also happy because the family had already decided that my failure at the fair was all Rufus' fault.

Emma brought the news. "Everyone is sorry they were hard on you.. In fact, they now realize you saved some sheep from drowning in the river." This was a big relief. I could let go of my shame, I could run, and herd sheep, and fall asleep easily at night, dog tired.

I saw Rufus now and then. He was busy helping Mr. Wilson find his sheep to get ready for shearing. We had no time to talk. I would have to set up a time for me to give him a piece of my mind, but I wasn't in a hurry. Rufus was larger than I was, and rather threatening.

Dad always hires shearers to do the work. Sheep don't always cooperate with the shearer, so these men need strong arms and endurance to go all day, apart from a few stops to rest. We live near the coast, and Derek finds his skilled shearers from there. They travel together, know each other well and are constantly telling jokes and stories. They liven up the place, I can tell you, but fortunately they drive home each night. Our house is not big enough for three or four noisy men, and our parents don't want Charlie or Summer to pick up their bad language either.

Some ranches are enormous, with many thousands of sheep, but ours operates on a much smaller scale – about 1,000 sheep and me the only herding dog. Dad couldn't afford to buy an assistant for me, so it was up to me to find as many sheep, including lambs, among the little hills and valleys on our property.

Fortunately there is a fence dividing the two ranches, but occasionally one or more sheep, being not very bright as I said before, would find a break in the fence and decide that the grass was greener on the other side. That made our job even harder.

All of the sheep were branded when they were young with the name of the ranch they came from. I heard dad tell mom that he preferred using less paint on each animal, just enough not to disappear in rainy weather, but not so much as to be permanent.

Joe Wilson's sheep were branded with minimal paint as well. This was very successful when Rosie and I used to round up his green branded animals from the Circle W Ranch and I took the purple ones that bore the name Coastal E Ranch. Some people think that all sheep look alike, but that's not true. Sheep farmers come to recognize at least some of their sheep and help each other with the troublemakers and the strays. We become a team. Not so for Rufus and me.

Dad looked worried after I sat at his feet, the signal that I'd finished my search. The yard was crowded with sheep, but dad had done a quick count. At that moment, Emma came by looking for me, and I heard him tell her that we were fifty sheep short of our total of 1,000.

Chapter 15 – Searching for Sheep

Having so many sheep missing was pretty serious. I don't know what sheep are worth, but from dad's dismayed look it must have been a lot. The wool from our farm is valuable – some is a sort of light grey; some is pure white. These particular fleeces are raised for the craft market. Spinning, weaving and so on, things that mom does and is very good at. Dad sells all of his fattened sheep for their meat. It's expensive and full of flavor. Our sheep and a few beef cattle now and then, support the ranch and the whole family. No wonder dad was upset. He got into his truck and waved Emma and me in.

"We'll go and look for the ones that are missing. I see that Rufus has not finished his roundup. That might help us if some of ours have found holes in the fence," he said.

But our search came up with only five with our purple ranch paint on them. Dad and I hustled them into the back of the truck. He didn't stop there, though.

He announced, "We'll have to keep going. I can't afford to lose the rest." As we left, it started to rain hard, and this worried dad even more. The wool should be dry before shearing.

We drove another half hour without seeing any more sheep. If this wasn't an emergency, I would have enjoyed the ride through oak trees that were pushing out new leaves. Heavy rain had fallen the previous week, and green grass was fast replacing the dry covering of winter and spring. Dad was not enjoying this trip. He stopped the truck and put his head in his hands. He was shaking. Just then I noticed in the distance another dog who was bringing a large flock toward us. It was Rufus of course. I put my paw on dad's shoulder and he looked up, amazed at what we saw.

Rufus looked exhausted. I understood why: these were long days. But something else caught my eye. He didn't seem to be herding them in the usual way. Instead he just walked along with the sheep. Now and then another would pop out from a behind a rock and join the others; sometimes one would disappear. Rufus' flock was a mass of purple and green paint and they were sopping wet and shivering. Dad's face turned bright red and his fists were clenched.

He yelled, "What are you doing, Rufus? You have a fine mix of sheep here, and some are mine."

I could tell that Rufus didn't understand. I went up to him and passed on dad's message. Nothing changed. Rufus just kept on walking, and told me to cool it. But I wanted to know more and after a few minutes he told me.

"This is a rotten place to work," he said, finally.

"Joe has way too many sheep. It's just too much. And I just know that when I get back he will beat me."

I felt sorry for him then. Sheep were going in all directions so I began sorting them into two flocks, ready to take ours back to the barn. Because I'd already found all except fifty, I thought I could manage the rest by myself, and I did. By dinner time, dad's tally was almost complete.

"Fantastic work, Sheila," he said, you're the best! We'll go out again tomorrow to find the last stragglers."

He walked to the fence to see if Rufus was back yet. Joe was standing outside, a can of beer in his hand.

"I see yours are home," he said. He looked angry. "Did you see Rufus on the trail?" I could see that dad was holding back a little, not wanting to boast.

"Well, yes," he said. "We did. He looked exhausted and the two brands were mixed together."

Joe was furious, and said, "Just wait until he gets back. I'll teach him a lesson!"

He went to his barn and brought out a stick. Emma and I looked at each other. She had picked up on my mood exactly, and said, "Mr. Wilson, I hope you don't beat him. That's not going to teach him anything except fear of you."

The old man walked off in a huff, muttering, "I paid good money for that dog and he's worthless."

Chapter 16 – KITTENS

I haven't mentioned Molly, our very pretty tabby cat. She's one of my best friends, especially now that Rosie has left. During the afternoon we were at the fair, Molly had gone. That's why I forgot to mention her sooner. I knew why she had disappeared, as she was looking rather fat. I didn't have to tell any of the others. Cyril announced that he knew about these things. She was about to give birth.

For a few days after that we were dying to see how many would be in the litter, and how many boys and how many girls. We loved guessing what Emma would name them.

At last the great day arrived. I'd been over at the Wilsons' fence, wondering how Rufus had managed the sheep, when Emma called to me and said, "Come and see, Sheila. Molly's had five beautiful kittens. They all look healthy. We won't know for a while

The kittens were all tabbies, like their mother, Molly

if they are male or female." I knew that. The kittens were all tabbies, like their mother, but the markings varied a bit.

"You'll have lots of fun playing with them," Emma told me. Because I'd never played with kittens, I decided to wait and see. Molly had been a stray, and this was her first litter at our farm.

Molly was stretched out on the ground, her tummy exposed. The kittens were fixed on her nipples and jostling each other, even though there was plenty of milk for all. They looked so tiny that I wasn't sure they'd survive.

Emma picked up one that had stopped drinking.

"It's so light," she said, her voice filled with wonder.

Mom came out, and said, "Emma, come and help me, would you please? We need to put Molly and the kittens in Summer's old Pack 'n' Play in your room. It's too noisy in the kitchen, and they can't be outside just yet."

"Great, mom, then I can check on them if I wake up in the night. Just imagine, I'll have six felines in my room. It's like a dream." They walked quickly back to the house.

I tagged along but was put off by all of the high-pitched mewing from the kittens. They just didn't stop, though surely they must have had to stop to sleep.

All day long there were visits from the family. I found myself getting a bit grumpy. Why should Molly and the kittens get all the attention? I turned my back on them and walked out.

Emma said, "Sheila, what's wrong?" I can't get away with anything when I'm around Emma. She came down the hall and looked at my face carefully.

"Are you just a little bit jealous?" I let my head bow down a bit, and she got the message.

"Now where is it? My photo album." She rummaged around for a minute or two, then opened a well-used book with shiny pages where you could put photos. She drew me to her and flipped through the book.

"Here you are, Sheila." She was pointing to a tiny puppy, whose coat was the same colors as mine, only in miniature.

"I was so happy when you were born, Sheila. I was about seven years old. The only sad part was that your mother died the following day. But you thrived. Now, Molly's kittens are exciting in the same way."

Emma took me back to the kittens' bed to watch the little creatures tumble over each other. They seemed cute to me now, and I began to look forward to playing with them when they'd grown a bit.

Chapter 17 – An Important Decision

Five weeks later, a lot had changed. The kittens were not yet weaned, and still needed some of their shots, but could play outside in the barnyard with Molly's supervision. Our favorite game was chase. I pretended to be asleep, then the kittens pounced on me, and I ran away with them chasing me. They never got tired of this game. Emma had named them Mittens, Lily, Luna, Momo and Taro: four girls and one boy. Mom and dad knew that Emma wanted to keep them all. I heard them discussing this one evening.

"Goodness, Lizzie. We already have a useless rooster who wakes us up at the crack of dawn." Mom was about to say something, but stopped as dad went on,

"A cow that doesn't produce any milk, four ducks that we'll never get to eat because Emma won't let us. A cat who does kill mice, but there aren't enough mice for six cats. We would be crazy to keep them all."

"But we have plenty of room, Derek, and Emma does so love animals," mom said. I was waiting nervously for their decision. Emma was asleep, so I was her eyes and ears. Just then a puff of wind came through the open window, and I sneezed loudly.

"Is that you, Emma?" asked mom. I came out of my hiding place under the stairs and walked up to her.

"And what do you think, Sheila? Should we keep all five?" She said this in a funny voice, as though she were speaking to a young child. What could I do? I can understand but not answer. It's so frustrating, and the funny voice is insulting as well. After a moment's thought I raised one paw, then the other, pretending to stretch them. Dad looked at mom in amazement.

"Does that mean two?" he said. "I know you sometimes think that Sheila can understand human speech, and I've always doubted you. And Emma, of course, says it's true. So what do you think now?"

"I have no idea," mom answered with a giggle. "But let's allow Emma to keep two kittens. This is the best answer we can give."

When Emma found out the next morning she was

at first sad, but after she'd spent a good deal of time thinking about which kittens to keep, and where the remaining three would go for adoption, she set about choosing two to stay. It turned out to be so difficult that in the end she had to decide by pulling names out of a hat. She kept Mittens and Lily.

It wasn't hard to find homes for the other three: in fact we found that the local SPCA had a waiting list for kittens. After they'd had all their shots, the other three would go to good homes. This would be several weeks away. In the meantime, Emma and I made the most of our time with the five little ones, and of course Molly, who was resting and feeling better every day.

Chapter 18 – Rufus' Story

After the shearing was done and I was praised for my herding skills, dad moved into the next task of ranch life: fattening the animals ready for sale in the fall. It was my job to do the reverse of what I'd done before shearing: herd them onto the pastures and let them go.

That done, it was time to confront Rufus about his behavior at the county fair. And while I was about it, I could scold him about his mishandling of the sheep. But now that the fair seemed so long ago, I decided that it would be more sensible to try to make friends with him. He did seem lonely at times, just wandering around in the yard. He didn't have the many friends I had in the barn. They were always ready for a chat. He didn't have a big family, just the Wilsons, and of course he couldn't understand what they were saying.

I found him sleeping under a tree near the fence where Rosie and I had spent many happy hours gossiping. When I put my paw on his head, he didn't react as I expected. He just opened one eye, looked at me, and closed it again.

"Come on, Rufus, get up and let's go for a run down to the mailboxes and see if there's mail. I bet I can beat you!" Rufus, who came with such a great reputation lifted his body up wearily, and said, "Who cares about the mailboxes. They can get it themselves." I was shocked at his selfishness, and replied, "Of course they can. They have legs. But don't you think it is an opportunity to thank them for bringing you to this lovely place? Wasn't it hard at your first home to share everything with other dogs? And how did the owners treat you? You looked in fine condition when you arrived."

I waited for Rufus to reply, and was very surprised to see him start to shake. A strange look came on his face; it was hard to pin down. Perhaps fear, or rage, or grief. He started running in circles and yelping as if in pain. I went closer and put one paw on one of his.

"It's all right, Rufus. You're safe now." I don't really know why I said that, over and over. It was the

There was no time to stop Rufus now

first thing that came into my head. I've always had good instincts and this time they fired up accurately. But Rufus didn't seem to notice that I was there. He was gone, somewhere in a memory that was upsetting to him. I said, "Nobody can hurt you now, Rufus." Then, "Look at me, Rufus! It's Sheila. I won't hurt you, and I'll work on Mr. Wilson so he won't beat you." It occurred to me then that I had approached him to give him a piece of my mind, and I smiled to myself. This conversation was turning out very differently than what I'd intended.

Suddenly he took off across the yard at top speed. I ran after him, but couldn't keep up. Soon he was out of sight. It dawned on me at that moment that he was heading for the river. He seemed obsessed with it.

Chapter 19 – REVELATIONS

After a while I spotted him again. He was slowing down and had nearly reached the river. My stomach dropped as I realized that he really meant to try to get away. But the crossing that looked easy was actually the top of a waterfall, and I blamed myself for not letting him know sooner. On the other hand, I still looked on him as an enemy, and maybe, just maybe, I forgot.

There was no time to warn Rufus now. He was at the edge of a little hill just above the waterfall. He didn't hear me over the sound of the rushing water, but he hesitated a bit, just long enough for me to jump on his back.

"Get out of here, can't you see the water? You'll drown if you try to get across." For a moment I thought he would jump anyway, but to my surprise he changed direction, skidded a bit on the bank and stopped right in front of me. His eyes were wild, he was panting and still shaking.

Gradually, bit by bit, his shaking grew less and less. He stood up straight and looked me in the eye with amazement.

"How did you know, Sheila?" At that moment I could have let him think I knew his story, but mom had always told all of us that honesty was important. So I admitted that my instincts were correct, but as to the story, I knew nothing. What were we to do now? I was worried that Rufus might feel embarrassed at falling apart the way he did, and he might clam up. I jumped in before he could say anything.

"You can tell me what happened if you want, and I'll be listening. I won't judge you. I'll support you. If you don't want to tell me, then we can put it aside for another time. But I hope you will choose to tell me. It can help take away the pain." He looked at me again and nodded, then surprised me by asking a question:

"What have you heard about the people who sold me to the Wilsons?"

"Not much, only that their dogs are bred carefully to be champions in their class, and that you came here sooner than expected because some other client pulled out at the last minute. I suppose the Wilsons heard the same story."

"That's what I thought, and it's a lie. All of us at that farm are mixes not purebreds. We have some shepherd in us but that's all. They only pick the ones who have markings close to yours. I presume you are a thoroughbred?" I nodded, but felt a little embarrassed. He went on. "A mixed dog with a coat similar to yours would fetch a very high price, though it would be rare to find a mixed breed dog with a full merle coat, like me. What I noticed first is that the adoptions always happened quickly due to a "cancellation." Mrs. Green would always offer to meet the buyer at the airport, for convenience. That meant that the new owners would not get to go to her place. If they had, they would have been shocked. We lived in dirty straw, ate horrible dog food, and we hardly ever went outside. Their certificates and stories of contests are fake. I suppose you heard that I am a champion?" His face was so sad, but I had to admit that he was right. He was starting to shake. Again, I put my paw on his shoulder, and he started to quiet down. His next comment was even more disturbing.

"I've noticed that you and the other animals here are never punished."

"That's true," I said. "My owners don't believe in it."

At that moment I sent grateful thoughts to mom and dad.

"It was very different at the farm. I won't describe the abuse, but you can probably imagine what it's like."

I nodded. Because I listen to every conversation I can lay my paws on, it's not unusual to hear sad stories like that, on radio or TV.

Rufus went on, "But all that changed when one of us was to be adopted. Suddenly the lucky one became the focus of Mrs. Green's attention. This is what happened to me before I flew out to be with Mr. Wilson. She took me on long walks, checked with the trainer that my herding skills were at least adequate, and made sure my body had no scars or other evidence of injuries. She fed me like a queen, for a week."

I could hardly believe my ears. My mind flashed back to the day that Rufus was late with the sheep due to exhaustion and frustration. Mr. Wilson had taken up a stick to punish him, but Emma had tried to talk him out of it. Now I understood why Rufus was so unfit to run all day; why he was not a skilled herder. He would never be the champion that the Wilsons had paid for. If Mr. Wilson treated him the same way as the adoption farm did, he would have a tragic life. I couldn't let that happen, but would need help. This would need careful thought. For the thousandth time, I wished I could talk.

Chapter 20 – A Plan

Many people, especially those who don't like dogs much, think we aren't very smart. I know that Emma thought I was smart, though she didn't know the whole truth about me. Mom and dad had an inkling about my abilities, but no one knew my big secret.

I spent a lot of time in the barn, just thinking. There had to be a way to let the Wilsons know that Rufus was not a purebred, why he didn't perform as they expected. Rufus had mentioned the certificates he'd supposedly won for his skills as a herder. They were fakes, he said.

A happy memory popped into my mind. A year or so ago Emma and I used to watch quiz shows on television. She named our game "Yes/No." When the contestant had to answer a question and Emma knew the answer, she taught me to bark once. If she didn't know the answer, I barked twice. We got pretty good at this, but it had been months since we'd played it. I'd have to take a chance, and hope that Emma would make the connection with the quiz show, and what I planned to do.

I'd probably have to have mom and dad there as well because Mr. Wilson was ignoring me, more than before. Put that down to jealousy. He wasn't a nice man. No wonder his daughter had rebelled all those years ago.

I'm known among the animals at the farm as being very patient. Waiting for dad, mom, Emma and the Wilsons to get together might not happen in my lifetime, but it was a bit more likely now that Mr. Wilson was seeing definite flaws in Rufus.

I played with the two remaining kittens for a couple of days. The other three had been adopted, and I could tell that my recommendation suited everyone.

Finally, the Wilsons were at the end of their rope with Rufus. It had been a blow to them that their supposed champion was way less impressive than they'd expected. Mom was right when she said that they were a competitive couple. They'd been taking Rufus to dog shows all over, even at a long distance. It was as though they needed to prove that the money they paid for Rufus was well spent. But there was no way that was going to happen.

Although our family didn't have much in common with the Wilsons, we were neighbors. They didn't seem to have any friends, and I'd heard mom and dad talk about a plan to have them to dinner. But they'd been putting it off because, they both agreed, there'd be nothing to talk about except Rufus.

Sheila hoped that Emma would remember
their game

🐾 🐾 🐾 🐾 🐾 🐾 🐾
Chapter 21 – THE TRUTH

At last, the Wilsons were so upset that they invited mom and dad to afternoon tea. We all knew that Edith, besides being a boring person, was an excellent cook, so dad accepted, knowing of course that they wanted his advice about what to do about Rufus.

I needed to be there to carry out my plan, and I needed Emma as well, although she knew nothing about it. It was my big chance. When Emma asked if she and I could come too, the answer was unexpected.

"Yes, that's all right, as long as they don't make a mess," said Edith. Whew! We'd never have gotten anywhere if we hadn't been allowed through the door.

When we had settled in, mom and dad on an uncomfortable couch, the Wilsons in their easy chairs and Emma and me on the floor, Edith started the conversation.

"It's a long time since a child has visited us. You know that our daughter is married now and has two little boys. She lives not far away, but we haven't seen the children at all. She says she's too busy." I noticed that she had tears in her eyes. Mr. Wilson gave her a hard look and she stopped. I saw mom and dad look at each other, but they didn't say anything. It wasn't our business of course, though I imagine it gave mom and dad information about how the Wilsons got along together, or didn't.

After a few awkward minutes when no one knew what to say, Edith went into the kitchen and brought out a large coffee pot and a plate of thick, warm brownies. Emma looked at me and wiped an imaginary tear from her eye. I can't eat chocolate – it might make me very sick; and she can't eat flour which has gluten in it, so we sat and watched the adults polish off the entire plate of brownies. Poor us.

Now the adults got down to business. Joe began with a list of ways that Rufus was a disappointment and not worth the money. Mom and dad looked surprised when they saw how long the list was. Joe, Edith and Rufus had traveled far and wide throughout the state, with some success, but not as much as the seller had promised. There was little improvement in Rufus' skills since the county fair several weeks before. And Joe reminded mom and dad about the dog's terrible performance in rounding up the sheep for shearing. Joe was getting angry and got up to show us the wall behind us, which was covered in big, colorful certificates, probably from the adoption agency. I guessed they claimed that Rufus was a champion. In one corner there were a few smaller ones, which he might have won since he arrived at the Wilsons' home.

Now it was time to take the biggest risk of my life. I had to rely on Emma to pick up on the clue I was giving. I had to hope that she remembered our quiz game. One bark would mean that the award was genuine, and two barks would mean it was fake. It was worth a try, but there was no guarantee of success. The Wilsons might just show us the door. They surely wouldn't permit too much barking in the house.

I realized that I had no idea which certificates were genuine and which were fake, because I can't read. But it wouldn't really matter, as all I had to do was push the Wilsons towards investigating what was going on with the breeders.

I was so nervous that I thought about pulling out. There were too many things that had to go right. But now that the brownies and coffee were gone, dad and mom might get up to leave at any minute. So I started my game. I looked at one of the large certificates on the wall and barked twice, then looked at Emma. She turned to me with a puzzled look. Then I picked another one and barked twice again, hoping that Emma would understand what I was doing. On the third run through I picked one of the smaller ones and barked once. She got it! Her eyes lit up, and she gave me a quick smile.

Finally, I chose one that looked pretty new, and barked only once. Mom and dad looked puzzled, and the Wilsons looked at each other and frowned, just as I stood before the largest and barked twice. Emma ran to me and hugged me. Then she looked around the room.

"Do you see what Sheila is doing?" she said. "She's showing us which awards are real and which are fakes."

"Fakes?" boomed Joe, "What are you talking about? It's ridiculous." He started muttering to himself. Edith just looked upset, but didn't seem to know what was going on. Dad chimed in,

"Joe and Edith, we all might think that dogs are not as bright as we are, but Lizzie and I happen to think that Sheila understands more about what is going on than you might think. We'll have to give it some thought, but at present I think this warrants a visit to the farm where Rufus was raised. Don't you agree? There's something fishy going on which could explain why he doesn't act like an Aussie. The blame might very well lie somewhere else."

The Wilsons looked stunned.

I expect that you've guessed what came next. The Merchants (us) and the Wilsons visited the abusive farm, unannounced, and were able to confirm what Rufus had told me.

There was a report to the police, arrests, and the business was closed. There was lots of publicity about Emma and me, even on the morning news programs.

We had our pictures in the paper, and we were given money for it. With the money, Emma bought Rufus.

The Wilsons were happy because they could now look for a real champion.

Rufus is getting fitter these days due to Emma's "exercise classes," which are mainly about running. He's even learning how to round up sheep, though not nearly as well as purebreds like me.

Visitors come to our farm to watch me, the senior Australian Shepherd and Alpha Dog; and Rufus, the Junior Mutt, doing our roundups. We work well together.

And we are best friends forever.

THE END

Afterword

This story grew out of a request from one of my granddaughters, eleven-year-old Isla, to write a book for her during the COVID-19 shelter-in-place restrictions in 2020. For once, I had time, as did she.

Isla had in mind who and what the plot should include. Her list of people included a family: mom, dad and four children with an age spread of fifteen down to 18 months. She named each member of the family and suggested details of their activities and character traits. Then she had a brain wave: why not include an Australian Shepherd dog who understands human language? We decided to go ahead with the project, using my choice of "Sheila" as the name for the dog.

Because we were separated for safety, we communicated via FaceTime. About once a week I sent her a few pages. She wasn't happy with any strife or discord; nor did she want her main child character,

12-year-old Emma, to play with dolls. The deer who found baby Summer in Sheila's dream could threaten her life only if he was not real.

Here's a bit about Isla. She's the middle child of three, a sixth-grader, and a true animal lover. Her interest in and vast knowledge of animals has grown over the years. She now fosters kittens for the SPCA prior to their adoption. Drawing is her other favorite activity: she's never bored when pens and paper are around.

Here's a bit about me. I am a licensed marriage and family therapist, mostly retired, the mother of three adult children and living with my husband in Davis, CA. I'm also the author of *Truth, Fiction and Lies*, a murder mystery set in Australia.

Isla's request delighted me. I've had so much fun writing this story. From the beginning I've had two goals: to produce a book that Isla will enjoy and treasure, and as a suggestion that other parents or grandparents might like to try during our weeks of confinement at home.

Finally, I am grateful to Marti Childs of EditPros in Davis, CA, who not only designed the interior and cover, but applied her usual calm and expertise to various problems that arose.

CPSIA information can be obtained
at www.ICGtesting.com
Printed in the USA
LVHW030809300720
661896LV00003B/117